# KUNBARRA AND THE WHITEANTS

# KUNBARRA AND THE WHITEANTS

A PORTIA OAKESHOTT, DINOSAUR
VETERINARIAN SHORT STORY

RAYMUND EICH

ISBN 9798844350405

First CV-2 Books trade paperback edition: August 2022


❦ Created with Vellum

# KUNBARRA AND THE WHITEANTS

The motorcoach rolled through the shadowed streets of the town at the bottom of the world.

That's what the advertising transponders called it, in between the times they hawked hotels, restaurants, and tourist attractions by pinging Portia Oakeshott's neuronal interface. Overlaid on her vision of one-story brick-fronted shops and smooth concrete sidewalks played videos of hot air balloon rides, a waterpark, the British history museum—all the sights in and around Blenheim. Except for the dinosaur preserve about thirty kilometers south of town.

At least the transponders knew she and everyone on the bus were dinosaur workers, not tourists.

Portia nestled deeper against the padded backrest. The seat's servos murmured to conform the padding to her body while a pop singer crooned in her mind's ear. Almost a full workday, ten hours on the bus to cross the thousand klicks from Port Bounty on the continent's north coast. The firewagon, some wit had called it when they'd boarded that morning. All hands on deck. The company's biggest rollout of dinosaur eggs in a decade.

Over a thousand, mostly mickeys and kunbarras, two similar herbivorous species covered with bony plates. The latest versions from the gene jocks had thicker egg casings and an instinct to bury them deeper into the preserve's rich soil, farther from the reach of small predators. Incubated to within a week of hatching at the company's Port Bounty headquarters, the eggs flew down earlier that day in the cargo holds of the company's biggest quadrotor aircraft, while the crews that would place the eggs in the field rode down. In comfort, yes, with snacks, tea, and coffee on demand from the esky and a well-ventilated loo for after the free drinks ran their course.

Still, a long day. Knowing only a couple of klicks remained in their journey made her impatient to get to the hotel. What took so long? Blenheim had an afternoon rush hour, believe it or not, but she'd driven through it before. Traffic shouldn't be as heavy as this.

The motorcoach turned. The brakes gave a pneumatic hiss. Her upper body swung a few centimeters off the backrest.

The bus came to a halt.

From the row in front of her, a field ecologist muttered, "What the bloody hell?"

She rolled her lips together at the indelicate language. Then something made her pause her music. A crowd's voices, words indistinct from distance and the motorcoach's insulated windows. A chant in a millennium-old rhythm of petulant protest.

Portia leaned forward and rested her hand on seat back in front. "Can you make out what they're saying?"

The field ecologist turned to her a face dominated by a high forehead and a pair of sunglasses. "Nah, Doctor."

She sat back and used her neury to pipe sound from the bus' external microphone to her auditory nerves.

The crowd's chant became clear. "Hey hey ho ho, dinos are abomino!"

She rubbed the side of her nose and darted glances around. Her coworkers in surrounding rows all had the look of listening in. All looked nervously to one another.

"Hey hey ho ho, dinos are abomino!"

The bus rolled a car-length forward, then stopped.

"Who the hell are they?" asked the field ecologist.

"Sounds like religious nutters, mate," said another male voice.

"Twenty-four-sevens?" the field ecologist said.

Portia spoke up. "No. To them, we're sinners because we don't keep Sunday of Earth's week as the sabbath. What we do with fossil evidence, bird and reptile DNA, simulations, and guesswork doesn't mean a whit to them."

The field ecologist looked over the back of his seat. Reflected in his sunnies were a hurricane fence and a nanotube alloy building frame. "Which religious nutters, then?"

Portia shrugged. "There's enough empty around here for a hundred cults to settle." Another thought came to mind. "Or maybe they came down from Port Bounty, or one of the big cities on Cookland."

"Hey hey ho ho, dinos are abomino!"

A third thought came. She shivered and pulled her arms together.

A dozen motorcoaches a day came into Blenheim during New New South Wales' weeks of summer. How did the protestors know this bus carried company employees? And to which hotel it traveled?

The motorcoach lurched forward, one car length at a time. The chant grew louder. She could make out the words through her own ears. Around her, her coworkers craned their necks to look for the protestors.

Another five meters forward. The chant broke up into ragged roar. A crowd fanned out along both sides of the bus. All wore plain clothes in shades of gray and black, sleeves to wrists, pants cuffs and skirt hems to ankles. Trimmed beards on the men. The women wore scarves knotted at the neck, covering their ears and most of their hair. Righteous anger distorted the faces of either sex. Men and women alike shook raised fists.

Louder than ever. "Hey hey ho ho, dinos are abomino!"

Portia pulled her arms tighter. Could they rock the bus over?

Blue and red lights flickered on the ceiling and the edges of headrests near the windows. The lights grew more intense, dancing on the sides of the protestor's faces. From somewhere behind the bus, a siren gave an abbreviated bark.

Protestors turned to look. The chant wavered.

Portia leaned toward the window and peered in the right direction, but couldn't see the source of the siren.

A deep voice boomed from a megaphone. "This is the City of Blenheim Police Department. Interfering with traffic on a public street is a violation of city ordinance. Remove yourselves to the sidewalk or you'll be arrested."

The chant stopped. Protestors looked to one another, to the police, and to one of their own. A man, he looked not much older than Portia, thirty standard at the most, and clad all in black. Dirty blond hair parted on the left, and hazel eyes holding a mix of fanaticism and shrewdness.

The man raised his hand and beckoned the protestors toward him. He opened his mouth. His voice, surprisingly gravelly coming from his smooth face, carried through the bus' insulated windows. "Brothers, sisters, we render unto Caesar. The Lord shall see us to triumph at the time of His choosing."

With measured steps, the protestors stepped back to the curb. Portia let out a long breath, though she still warily watched the crowd. The anger recently on their faces had turned, but how quickly could it turn back?

Then she saw a woman with green eyes. Wisps of coal-black hair peeped under her scarf. The lines of her cheekbones, the upturned nose, she looked familiar. From uni? That girl who lived down the hall in Portia's final year. What was her name? Sally? Sandra.

Portia's nose wrinkled. Sandra had been a girl of colorful, skimpy attire and questionable virtue. Rumor had it she'd sneaked a boy into her room one night when her roommate was away. That couldn't be her, in a dour dress, four thousand klicks and three standard years from campus.

Could it?

The bus rolled forward. The chant resumed, louder than before. Sandra stood next to the man in black. They and the others watched the bus go with unreadable eyes.

· · ·

THE NEXT MORNING, protestors lined the street as the motorcoach left the hotel, bound for the field office amid farmland two klicks south of Blenheim. Portia studied the crowd but Sandra eluded her eye.

That she'd seen her classmate she lacked all doubt. The night before, keyed up and unable to fall asleep, she searched the alumni forum. A year prior, Sandra Nithercott had changed her profile picture. No makeup, gray dress and scarf. *I've set aside my sins and found peace and joy with the Siblinghood.* The profile stated she lived in a small town in the Bagehot Hills of northern Blighland, eight hundred klicks from here.

More searching found a page about the Siblinghood. The commune eked out its quid by handcrafting pottery and wooden furniture, under the spiritual leadership of Brother Lucas Ruthven. A photo showed Ruthven in black and with dirty blond hair parted on the left.

One mystery solved, but another came to mind.

Why did the Siblinghood protest the company?

The bus pulled in at the field office, and a third mystery pressed out her other concerns. A sport ute in Blenheim PD colors parked with blinking lights near a windowless, two-story building of corrugated metal near the back of the grounds. The hangar. Yellow crime scene tape wrapped the building, with an extra strip of tape across the rolling doors.

"What did those mangy bastards do now?" muttered the field ecologist with the sunnies.

After debarking, they soon found out from the field office's operations manager. During the night, someone had stolen the rotors of every quaddy in the hangar. Neatly dismantled and removed, not just from the hangar, but from the entire grounds. The quaddies wouldn't fly until replacements were fabbed and remounted. The latter had to wait for the police forensics team to hoover up every scrap of evidence.

From the back of the crowd, Portia squinted across the grounds. Black half-domes of cameras dotted the hangar. "Surely we have video of the perpetrators," she called out.

The operations manager shook his jowly head. "The grounds lost main power last night. The backup generator failed to kick in. We found all the lines severed this morning. The police think the hood-lums used drones to knock out power, then did their work."

Power knocked out for hours. Portia gasped. "The kunbarra eggs!"

"Were covered in self-adjusting insulation. They stayed within temperature tolerances even with the loss of controlled ambient. We're a little cross at the overnight vet in the incubator for sleeping through everything." A wry smile softened the words. "Luckily, no one and no eggs were hurt."

A man's nasal voice barely carried from the front of the crowd. "It's obviously the religious fanatics what did this."

The ops manager rubbed the bags under his eyes. "Obviously, but the police still have to gather proof."

"When can we deploy the eggs?" asked the field ecologist with the sunnies and high forehead.

"We'll push for today, but if I were a punter, I'd bet against it. We ordered rotors from the municipal fab, right. But we have to wait for the police to finish before the mechanics can get started. Then the quaddies need test flights before the mechanics will cert them for use." He gave a grin. "But I reckon we can find a task around here for every jack and jill of you."

He was right. For a few hours. But by seventeen o'clock, local noon, Portia had finished checking the dispensary for expired medication. She joined the rest of the crew milling about on the parking lot and adjoining lawn. Some of the men played cricket with a broom and a ball made from duct tape. A glance past them, into the hangar, showed mechanics climbing up ladders and disassembling rotor housings. Strangers, bulky men wearing untucked shirts, swiveled their heads, ignoring the company employees, their gazes on the perimeter fence.

Between bowled balls, an ecologist playing deep midwicket told her in a scratchy voice, "Hired security. Company flew them in from Centennial City an hour back. They'll be on-site round the clock."

The ops manager's voice called across the parking lot from the front steps of the main building. "Hullo, what's this?"

The batsman shrugged with the broom in his hands. "We're all done with our tasks."

"You're all—" Even from a distance, the ops manager's jowly face showed surprise. "Crikey. Right, here's an update. The mechanics just informed me they need two flights eighteen hours apart to cert each quaddy. They cannot get that done today. So we're sending you back to the hotel."

Cheers sounded from the cricket players. Two blocks away, the motorcoach turned the corner for the field office.

"Don't get too much a gutful tonight. The motorcoach will pick you up tomorrow at twelve-thirty, and God help you if you're late."

Everyone filed aboard in good spirits. Who didn't want a paid day off? The kunbarra eggs wouldn't hatch for a few days yet. Fly them out tomorrow. No chant could stop a quaddy.

A chill ran down Portia's throat.

Would the Siblinghood escalate from chants to homemade missiles?

The bus rolled out the gate. On the far side of the road, against a backdrop of a hops field, eight Siblinghood members stood like ghosts in black and gray. Silent till now, they chanted in unison. Their voices lingered in Portia's mind long after the bus moved out of earshot.

More protestors waited for them at the hotel. They formed two lines flanking the entryway, barely farther apart than the bus was wide. The bus crept past contorted faces less than half a meter from Portia's window. The chant sounded louder than ever. "Hey hey ho ho, dinos are abomino!"

Heart racing, she scanned the faces for Sandra Nithercott, but didn't find her.

Finally, the motorcoach squeezed through the protestor gauntlet. Blenheim PD and more private security, hired by the company or the hotel, stood in clusters of two or three on the parking lot. They all looked to be suffering heartburn as their gazes roved the protestors.

The bus pulled up under the front awning. A company employee, a mousy woman with plump cheeks, waited for them. Her voice carried surprisingly well. "I'm beaming each of you a twenty cryptoquid voucher good for the hotel's restaurant and lounge."

The man with the nasal voice spoke. "You're telling us we have to stay on site?"

"You're grownups. We can't make you stay here. But with twenty quid in your pocket, why go anywhere else?"

The employees strode in. A typical lobby of a small town hotel, plastic plants, a bored young woman looking up in surprise from the front desk, a freshwater aquarium instead of a fountain. Most of the crowd headed left, toward the bar. Portia veered to the right.

"Doctor." The field ecologist had pushed his sunnies up his high forehead. He waggled his wrist as if it held a glass. "Having a pint?"

She smiled politely. "Not just yet. I need to look something up."

In her room, she sprawled on the bedspread and gazed idly at an impressionist print of kangaroos on the wall above the headboard. She rolled her lips together once. A good idea?

What harm could come of it?

Portia nodded to herself, then dictated a message through her neury.

*To: sandra.nithercott@alumni.ueb.edu.nnsw*

*I got quite the surprise, looking out the bus window yesterday and seeing you here in Blenheim. Would like to know more about your position and tell you more about mine. Free today?*

[Send,] she told her neury through nerve impulses rerouted away from her voicebox.

She waited for ten minutes, until a rumble in her stomach reminded her to eat lunch. In the hotel restaurant, she sat with a caprese salad. The balsamic vinegar lacked punch but the basil leaves surprised her with freshness. She washed down a bite with a sip of hot tea when an alert popped up in the lower right corner of her vision. *New message from sandra.nithercott@alumni.ueb.edu.nnsw.*

Portia opened it and read.

*I thank the Lord our paths have crossed. Brother Lucas and I would love to meet you. We've camped at a ground east of town.* A virtual card gave the full address, down to the site number. *Can you come to us this evening, twenty-six o'clock?*

She sipped her cuppa, composed her reply.

*Till then.*

. . .

AT HALF PAST TWENTY-FIVE, after changing out of her company uniform, she stopped in the hotel lounge and told people she was heading off site for a couple of hours. She gave the campground address.

"What's there?" asked a woman with the precise enunciation of the mostly drunk.

"The Siblinghood. The protestor cult."

The man with the nasal voice cut in. "Why'n the bloody hell are you visiting the enemy?"

"Don't I destroy my enemies when I make them my friends?"

Portia went to the back of the hotel. The door recognized her as a hotel guest and unlocked itself. Her rideshare waited on a strip of living asphalt facing the tall wooden privacy fences backing a residential neighborhood. She walked around the entire car. A nondescript sedan with the side and rear windows tinted dark.

She tossed a clutch purse onto the front seat, then climbed in and curled up next to it. Below line of sight of any casual glance through the windshield. The scents of new car and vat-grown leather comforted her.

The sedan rolled around the hotel. Seen through the tinted windows, the private security men watched the parking lot entrance and didn't give her a second glance.

A block away, Portia moved to the rear seats and sat up for the rest of the ride to the campground. The evening sun sent the car's shadow ahead of her. The sedan slowed, making her frown in puzzlement. A line of sweetgum trees screened the facility's entrance from the road.

A paved lane led past a concrete block building housing the front desk and gift shop. A teenaged boy wearing a polo shirt with the campground logo stood on the pavement and raised his hand. He leaned down and from under a sheaf of disheveled brown hair peered at her. Neury to neury, he said, [Checking in or visiting?]

[Visiting.]

The boy grimaced. [We won't stop you, but mind, we don't want trouble coming in or going out.]

[I'll give you none. Which way to site 14?]

His grimace remained as he gave directions and pointed. He stepped aside and the sedan rolled on. A left turn, then past RVs parked on gravel and down a hill toward a gully. Along the bank, branches of oaks and maples rustled over rows of tents.

She studied everything. No telling what detail might be important to help the company overcome the Siblinghood. *And bloody hell, record what you see and hear to your neury.* She gave the commands and heat drained from her cheeks.

Just past a concrete block building with signs for mens' and womens' and the guest laundry, two men in gray and black stopped her car. The one with the slender build and crewcut spoke. [Your name and your purpose?]

[Portia Oakeshott. I'm here to visit—there she is.]

Sandra glided toward them, her skirts rustling the pavement. "I've invited her to meet Brother Lucas," she said, voice warm. Her green eyes met the gaze of the crewcut guard. A private conversation over their neuries, obviously.

Sandra turned to Portia. "Park here, then come with me."

Portia did as bade, then climbed out, clutch purse in hand. The summer air felt warm on her bare elbows and her ankles exposed by her crop pants. How could Sandra stand being smothered in her thick, dark skirts?

"You look good," she said, to say something. A closer look and then she noticed a glow in Sandra's full cheeks.

Sandra beamed. "You see it. The Lord has blessed me with a healthy pregnancy, so far."

A glance down, no baby bump. "How far along?"

"Three standard months." Sandra's green eyes crinkled. Her gaze darted to Portia's bare ring finger. "No children for you yet?"

"We have hundreds of kunbarra eggs to lay out on the preserve."

Sandra's smile dripped sweet condescension. "In time you'll find that isn't remotely the same." She scratched under her head scarf, just above her ear, and Portia recalled she'd often worn jangling hoop earrings. "I remember you were a veterinary major, but what led you to work on dinosaurs?"

Her tone gave Portia pause. She hadn't thought about Sandra's agenda, but now it seemed obvious. Gather intel from Portia, if not convert her outright. So Portia set aside the true answer—a childhood playing with plastic dinos in her suburban bedroom had planted the seed of a passion—and said with a rueful tone, "The pay is good."

"And?"

"My then-boyfriend took a job with the company. I followed because I thought we loved each other."

Sandra's mouth opened as if to ask further. Sweat trickled in Portia's underarms and she wished she'd applied more anti-perspirant from the tiny stick in her clutch purse. God willing Sandra wouldn't pry for more details on which young man at uni had been her non-existent boyfriend.

"The only love which never wavers is the Lord's. Here we are."

The tent looked like a small house with guy lines. Angled sunlight through the trees gave a glow to panels of yellow and orange. From the panels, Portia judged the tent had two side rooms off the main. An LED lantern hung unused over the door, which dangled loosely in the breeze. Coiled flaps let air into screened windows.

Another guard stood midway between a cold firepit and a canopy over a picnic table. His pendulous ears wobbled as he turned his head to Sandra. "This is her?"

"Yes, brother."

He set his hands on his hips and jutted out his elbows. He narrowed his eyes at Portia, but after a moment his expression softened. "The Lord faults no one for ignorance. Brother Lucas will speak to you of truth." He stepped aside and turned. With one hand he gestured toward the tent.

Portia walked that way over dirt and patchy grass. The guard's gaze never left her face. Her fingers tightened on her clutch purse. She would almost prefer the guard's eyes dart to her figure, as every man, no matter how pious, was wont to do from time to time.

She kept her thoughts off her face and went by the guard with a single nod of her head.

Sandra stepped around Portia and pulled the door flap back about five centimeters. "Brother Lucas?" she said through the gap, voice soft and warm.

Lucas Ruthven cleared a little gravel from his throat, but not much. "Enter, little sister, and Dr. Oakeshott."

Sandra held the flap fully open. Portia entered without needing to stoop. Her grip tightened on the clutch purse. Her coworkers knew her location and police forensics caught every criminal. Still, she entered a lion's den.

Ruthven stood near the back of the tent with his hands behind his back. His hazel eyes regarded her and how much gel did he put in his dirty blond hair to keep his part so sharp all day?

*Set aside your nerves and focus on what's important.*

"G'day, Doctor."

Portia extended her hand. "G'day, Mister—Reverend—Brother—?"

"Brother Lucas, if you please." Ruthven gave her hand a cool look. "No offense, but other than in service to the Lord, I touch no woman but my wife."

Portia dropped her hand and gave a gracious smile. "I respect your ways, Brother Lucas." Inwardly, she seethed. As if *she* were a harlot lusting after *him*.

To cover her thoughts, she glanced toward a sound from the side room to her left. Someone shifting his or her body. For a moment, a bright shaft of sunlight threw a silhouette onto the orange plastic wall. Mannish shoulders, close-cropped hair, upturned nose and bearded jaw. Obviously not Ruthven's wife.

Then who?

Ruthven cleared his throat. He extended his hand toward a stool near the door and two steps to Portia's left. "Doctor, have a sit, if you please."

Portia took a seat on a thin cushion. Though slender as styluses, the stool's nanotube alloy legs held her weight. Sandra sat on a stool to the right of the door. Ruthven lowered himself to one near the back wall. The three of them formed a triangle facing one another. Portia's nape crawled with the realization that someone lurked no more than two meters behind her.

"What brought you to visit us, Doctor?"

Portia gestured at Sandra. "I looked out the window yesterday and saw a familiar face." She turned to Ruthven's hazel eyes. "It made me want for us to get to know each other better. Perhaps we can find some common ground—"

"We cannot compromise with sin, Doctor."

She blinked. "I, your words, what exactly do you mean that 'dinosaurs are abominations'?"

"The meaning should be plain to one of my little sister's uni classmates."

"Yes, I suppose, what I mean, what makes them abominations or sins?"

"They are abominations because they are the fruits of your sins. You play god and the Lord will pass judgment. I pray that you repent before His judgment falls on you."

Portia rubbed the side of her nose. "I understand our techniques might be unfamiliar to the general public, but perhaps if I explain—"

"No explanation is needed," Ruthven said. "I majored in livestock science at North Blighland A & M. I well know all the techniques used in genetic engineering and ecoseeding."

"I don't understand."

"The Lord ordained that dinosaurs should pass from the universe sixty-five million years ago. Your company usurp the Lord's prerogative to decide which species live and which pass away. Do you understand now?"

Portia drew in a deep breath. Despite the smells of tent plastic and castile soap, her heart slowed and slid down from her throat. "I do."

Ruthven's hazel eyes softened. "Are you happy, Doctor?"

"Frankly, no. Come visit the preserve. I'll contact my superiors, perhaps a private guided tour. If you see them up close—"

"Not that," he said with a wave of his fingers. "Are you pleased living the life the king of the world tells you to live?"

She frowned. "What's Arthur II to do with anything?"

"The king of the material world, who took the Whore of Babylon as his consort." With a touch of exasperation, he said, "Satan."

Portia shuddered. "I live a Christian life."

Ruthven scowled. He opened his mouth to speak when Sandra leaned forward. "Brother Lucas, if I may?"

"Yes, little sister."

Sandra turned to Portia. Her head scarf framed her green eyes and her face lacking guilt and shame. "I know you didn't commit sins of the flesh in our uni days, and you look too much a lady for me to imagine you commit them now. Brother Lucas is instead talking about all the false things our society demands of you. You must get good grades. You must go to uni. You must find a good husband who has a good job. You must raise your children to repeat the cycle. And at the end, you wonder why your kitchen full of gadgets and your winter weeks at Capricorn Beach fail to make you happy."

She went on. "Strewth, they don't make anyone happy. Though the rich men who cannot pass through the eye of the needle fatten their cryptoquid accounts off you, they cannot fill the emptiness inside. And the men with reversed collars under vaulted ceilings and stained glass windows, who tell you the false things are God's will, feel their emptiness so much they secretly deny God exists. Why listen to them when you can listen to Brother Lucas?"

Portia's head swam in the stuffy air of the tent. Her head thrashed from Sandra to Ruthven and back. Sandra lied, of course. Ruthven was the man who demanded false things and claimed God wanted them. He had to be. Everything here had the sulfurous stink of a cult.

"You say so much," she said. "I really must go. Thank you for your hospitality but I really must go." On a hunch, she lowered her hand with the clutch purse below the seat of the stool and let go.

"Stay, sister. My words are a kookaburra's call compared to the truths Brother Lucas can tell you."

"No, I must, my coworkers, they know I'm here, I don't want them calling the police if I'm away too long—"

"You're free to go," said Ruthven in his gravelly voice. "And free to come back at the time of your choosing."

Sandra bowed her head to him. "You are indeed wise, Brother Lucas." She extended her arm and took Portia's hand. "Come, sister, I'll walk you to your car."

Portia followed Sandra out. Rows of tents stretched up the slope toward the restroom and laundry building. The guard with the pendulous ears gave Portia a wistful look. She gave him a smile to make her grandmother proud, then walked away.

How long should she wait?

Sandra helped her answer the question. Halfway to the waiting sedan, Sandra's mouth scrunched and a pained expression touched her green eyes. She rested her hand on her stomach. "I don't know why they call it morning sickness. It can strike anytime."

"That'd be right," Portia said. In a quiet voice, she added, "Oh dear."

"What's the matter?"

"You might suffer from some nausea, but at least you're free of the monthlies."

Sandra's eyes went wide with sympathetic understanding. "You don't take hormones to regulate or prevent it? That's pleasing to the Lord."

Portia looked down at her hands. "And I carried along—just in case —where did I leave my clutch?"

"You had it with you when we entered Brother Lucas' tent. Didn't you?"

"I did. I must have left it there." Her mouth turned down and she swung her head from Sandra to the tent down the slope.

"Go get it." Sandra winced and flattened her fingers on her mouth. "I can't go with you." She turned for the womens', her usual poise lost to shuffling feet and torso hunched over her stomach.

One of her handlers down. Portia went back downslope. A gaggle of low clouds masked the rays of Stella Australis A. In the slight gloom under the oaks' spread branches, the guard with the pendulous ears opened his mouth in a smile. "What brings you back, miss?"

"I was so engrossed by Brother Lucas' message that I forgot something. Mind if I go in and get it? Half a tick and I'll be out of his way."

"Of course. His messages engross us all."

Portia gave a half-smile over her shoulder. She approached the tent. The door flap was still unzipped. Soundlessly, she lifted it and stepped over the thin plastic threshold into the shaded interior, prepared to apologize to Ruthven for interrupting—

He wasn't in the main room.

She glanced around. Her clutch purse there, under her stool.

In which side room was Ruthven?

"She gives us an in to the company." His gravelly voice came from the left.

"Whatever." A harsh male voice with an odd, flat accent. Not from New New South Wales. Not even from any of the can-worlds and space stations in the Stella Australis system. "Tomorrow you start protesting the high-end hotels. Especially the Churchill, that's where most off-worlders stay. Make rich bitches clutch their pearls."

"If we work on the company's employees, we can further your objective and save their souls."

Portia picked up her purse and backed away.

The male voice grew harsher. "Who's paying your bills here—" He switched to an exaggerated strine accent. "—*mate*?"

With a faint rustle, her back and rump pushed aside the loose door flap. She held her breath until she lifted both her feet over the threshold and onto bare ground. She turned and strode quickly away.

"All's good?" the guard asked.

Portia waggled her purse, then touched a finger to her lips. "Brother Lucas is resting," she said softly.

The guard lowered his voice. "Right good of you to tell me."

"G'day," she said, and hurried up the slope. There, just past the restrooms and the two guards, her rideshare sedan. Get in, get out of here, before someone suspects.

A retching sound echoed off concrete block and out the doorway to the womens'. Sandra.

Portia's fingers stiffened around her clutch. What might Sandra tell Ruthven? *She said she had an urgent feminine issue. I'm surprised she rode back to her hotel to address it.*

Though part of her wanted to sprint to the rideshare, Portia over-came the urge. With quick steps, she entered the womens'. Beyond the mirror, sinks, and handsoap dispensers, Sandra's retching reverberated out of the first stall. Portia went to the last stall, giving a glance to the only window on the back wall, high, small, two panels of frosted glass of which one could be leaned out. Perhaps a gymnast or a lady spy could slip through, but she couldn't.

Portia closed the stall door behind her. Her nose wrinkled at the bite of bleach undercut by a mildewy odor from the showers. She crouched, not letting the seat of her pants touch the toilet. Her quads burned, but at least someone seeing her feet under the stall partition would assume she sat.

How long would it take to sell her story? She braced her hands, one on the concrete block wall and the other on the metal stall partition, until the burn in her quads forced her to stand.

With a tight feeling in her gut, she left the stall. None of Ruthven's guards blocked the entrance. Only Sandra, bent over a sink, shared the restroom with her.

Sandra straightened up. Water dripped down her pallid cheeks. She reached for a recyclable cloth handtowel that muffled her words as she blotted her face. "The Lord only made us bear these burdens to bring new life into the world because He knew we could manage them."

Portia smiled weakly. Quick bursts of water, soap, more water. She wrung a towel through her hands. If only she could ask Sandra about the man with the flat accent... but that would give the game away. "I wish you and your husband all the best with your baby."

"Please, sister, mind Brother Lucas' words. He speaks the truth, and happy are all those who hear."

"I will," Portia said. "G'day."

Two minutes later, the rideshare turned out of the campground's driveway and onto the main road back to Blenheim. A glance behind her showed no one followed. She gave a relieved sigh and pulled excerpts from her neury recording. As the sedan approached a half-completed development of new houses raised on stilts Queenlander style, she rang up John Pietrangelo, the company's chief operations officer.

Ten seconds for the call to bounce off a satellite and reach Port Bounty. A video window appeared between her and the sedan's windshield. Black hair low on his forehead, a lean and sharp face, wiry limbs. A tall boy on the schoolyard had probably mocked his short stature. Once.

A gray suit, a knotted yellow tie, and a bookcase behind him filled with golf memorabilia showed Pietrangelo was still in his office despite the late hour. "You aren't one to jump the chain of command willy-nilly, Dr. Oakeshott. What's come up?"

Her heard thumped. "I paid a visit to the Siblinghood's leaders."

"You did what?"

"I saw a familiar face among the protestors, an acquaintance from uni. I contacted her and she introduced me to the Siblinghood's leader."

He glanced to the side, checking data through his neury. "Lucas Ruthven?"

"Yes."

Black eyebrows knitted. "A moment ago you said 'leaders.'"

A smile pushed tight her cheeks. "I recorded some things you need to see. And hear."

"Send them."

She transferred the silhouette and the conversation between Ruthven and the man from outsystem. Pietrangelo sipped from a black mug of coffee and stared intently past her. "That's an American accent.... If it's from… I'll be stuffed."

Glinting dark eyes focused on Portia. "Good onya for finding this. I've got a hunch. I'll run this through an accent checker."

A moment later, Pietrangelo's eyes squeezed shut and he threw back his head. He guffawed from deep in his belly. "Mangy whiteant bastards!"

"Sir?"

His laughter died down enough to talk. "We called it 'whiteanting' where I grew up, around Anzac Cove. You don't know the word?"

"No."

"It's when someone plays unfair to bring down the competition. Hiring someone to post one-star reviews of your rival's products, things like that." Pietrangelo chuckled. "That bloke's wank-yank accent matches to New Minnesota."

"New Minnesota." Her eyebrows jumped. "Plastocine Park."

"Now, now, let's take the high road and call it by its proper name, 'Pleistocene Park.'"

She'd seen videos, of course. Sabertooth tigers prowling around herds of woolly mammoths. Hagerman horses galloping across a plain. Short faced bears, taller than a man, attacking giant tapirs. All running loose on a small continent, all reconstructed in part from preserved DNA. All extinct.

"They do the same thing the Siblinghood condemns us for." She didn't laugh but simply shook her head. "Mangy whiteant bastards, indeed."

"I'll forward this on to the Frontier Police. From the silhouette and the voice print, they can likely identify that bloke."

"And arrest him."

Pietrangelo grimaced. "Wager you five quid he's diplomatic personnel attached to the New Minn embassy. The frontos and I will have to lobby the Foreign Minister to have the bloke declared *non grata*. But that's not what's important."

"It isn't?" Portia asked.

"Not compared to knocking out Lucas Ruthven's cult."

"I see. He'd lose all credibility with his followers." Her voice sounded quiet in her ears. Cult or not, Sandra seemed happy enough with her new life.

"Who cares about them? Ruthven's credibility with tourists, especially off-worlders, will get smashed flat. That's all that matters."

"If I may, sir. No."

"No?"

She thought of newborn kunbarras, cracking their eggs open from the inside with pushes of their blocky heads. "What most matters is our dinos."

# ABOUT THE AUTHOR

I'M RAYMUND EICH. I use my Middle American upbringing as a launchpad for journeys to the ends of the Universe.

Growing up in the Midwest prepared me for my academic career, culminating with a Ph.D. in biochemistry from Rice University. It helps me help inventors prosper from their progress in medicine, biotechnology, and computer hardware.

Above all, it inspires me to write science fiction and fantasy about ordinary people facing extraordinary wonders and horrors, battling enemies both foreign and domestic, and building better lives for themselves, their families, and their societies.

My last name has one syllable and is pronounced "eye-sh." I live in Houston with my family.

Connect with me at **www.raymundeich.com** or follow the QR code below.

Online and brick-and-mortar bookstores around the world list millions of books, with thousands more published every day. I'm glad you discovered this one.

If you'd like to know when I release a new book, instead of leaving it to chance, join my Readers Club. I'll email you every two weeks with publishing news, book recommendations, or a short personal update.

**Yes, please!** I'll go to **www.raymundeich.com/mailing-list** or scan the QR code below.

No thanks. I'll take my chances next time I look for your books.

# OTHER BOOKS BY THE AUTHOR

Available wherever books are sold.

Learn more about these titles at our website, **www.cv2books.com,** or follow
the QR code below.

# Portia Oakeshott, Dinosaur Veterinarian

As a girl, Portia Oakeshott dreamed of caring for the reconstructed dinosaurs roaming the preserve near the south pole of her hot home planet, New New South Wales.

As a graduate from the planet's top veterinary school and a recent hire by the dinosaur company, caring for dinosaurs brings Portia into conflict with ranchers, spoiled children, villainous millionaires, religious fanatics, and politicians. Her adventures take her from the "big smoke" to the "back of Bourke"—from the bustling city of Port Bounty, across a continent of vast fields where farmers raise pigs containing cloned human organs, to the lush Cretaceous forests at the bottom of a world.

## Riddlepigs and the Cryla

As a new hire at the dino company, Portia's first call sends her to an isolated farmhouse and across the perimeter into the preserve itself, in pursuit of a rogue carnivore, a female *Cryolophosaurus*. A cryla.

Amid a forest of ferns and cycads, Portia learns a lesson never taught by her professors at veterinary school. A lesson in what "caring for dinosaurs" really means.

## Minnie and the Trekker

Today, caring for dinosaurs means tending a female *Minmi*—a minnie— mindlessly tending a clutch of eggs smashed and devoured by an unknown predator.

Back at base, caring for dinosaurs means identifying the predator. Before it wreaks more havoc on the fragile ecosystem of the preserve.

## Winner and the Poacher

As a consultant to law enforcement, Portia confronts stark evidence of a rich young man's crime: the mounted head of a massive herbivorous *Wintonotitan*. A winner.

A dinosaur the company never granted a permit for hunting.

Journeying to the bottom of the world in the sunless week of latewinter, Portia and a policeman must unravel a web of sins and lies to build an airtight case.

And survive the desperate acts of the guilty.

*<u>Coming Soon</u>*

**Loovy and the Lava**

# Novels

## The Progress of Mankind

*Stone Chalmers, Book 1*
*Complete four-book series available*

Stone Chalmers. Spy. Assassin. Instrument maintaining Earth's dominion over all human worlds.

Opposing him? Hostile forces on colony worlds… and within the Earth government itself.

~

## Take the Shilling

*The Confederated Worlds • Book 1*
*Complete trilogy available*

Tomas seeks an escape from his backwater planet and his widowed mother's rigid religious home.

'Taking the shilling' - enlisting as a space soldier - is only the start.

## The Blank Slate

Neuroscience entrepreneur Clay Shieffer must stop a tyrannical president...
because he unwittingly gave the tyrant power over the human mind.

## New California

After New California's founder committed suicide, two men vied to rule the
colony.

Ashwin George, supported by the colony's elite and the Chinese company
dominating half the settled galaxy.

Against him, Desmond Park, nanotechnology engineer, armed with the most
formidable weapon of all.

A single idea.

## The Reincarnation Run

Skeptical spacejock Landry Krieger knows exactly how to smuggle the
"reborn" spiritual leader of an oppressed people past their conquerors... but
the boy's priests—and governess—shake up his orderly plans.

## Azureseas: Cantrell's War

Ross Cantrell joined the animal control mission on the newly-discovered
planet Azureseas to earn the money to start married life together with his
girlfriend.

Then Ross discovers the truth about the planet's "animals."

## Short Novels

### Love and Death in the City of Bone

*He had a month to learn the planet's mysteries—and Juliette's.*

His cover story: return to Elard to dismantle his sect's missionary work to the planet's natives.

His true mission: investigate decades-old mysteries of love and death.

His objective: return to Earth with his discovery.

If he can.

### A Mighty Fortress

Theodore and his team from the Lutheran Interstellar Terraforming Society would transform a barren, rocky world into a refuge of faith and life.

Or die trying.